SACRAMENTO PUBLIC LIBRARY

D0100030

Jodie's Passover Adventure

BY ANNA LEVINE   ILLUSTRATED BY KSENIA TOPAZ

KAR-BEN
PUBLISHING

For my parents, Ruth and Wilfred.

Thanks to great friends who join me on adventures. And my wonderful family,

Alex, Nimrod and Tomer who encourage me to keep exploring. – A.L.

To my amazing daughters, who always stand by me, both as family and as

the most truthful reviewers of my work. – K.T.

Text copyright © 2012 by Anna Levine
Illustrations copyright © 2012 by Lerner Publishing Group

All rights reserved. International copyright secured. No part of this book may be
reproduced, stored in a retrieval system, or transmitted in any form or by any means–
electronic, mechanical, photocopying, recording, or otherwise without the prior written
permission of Lerner Publishing Group, Inc., except for the inclusion of brief quotations
in an acknowledged review.

Kar-Ben Publishing
A division of Lerner Publishing Group, Inc.
241 First Avenue North
Minneapolis, MN 55401 U.S.A.
Website address: www.karben.com

Library of Congress Cataloging-in-Publication Data

Levine, Anna (Anna Yaphe)
    Jodie's Passover adventure / by Anna Levine ; illustrated by Ksenia Topaz.
       p. cm.
    Summary: Amateur archaeologist Jodie invites her cousin Zach on an adventure
exploring Hezekiah's Tunnel in Jerusalem when he comes for a visit over Passover.
    ISBN 978-0-7613-5641-7 (lib bdg. : alk. paper)
    [1. Hezekiah's Tunnel (Jerusalem)—Fiction. 2. Cousins—Fiction. 3. Jews—
Jerusalem—Fiction. 4. Jerusalem—Fiction.] I. Topaz, Ksenia, ill. II. Title.
PZ7.L57823Jo 2012
[E]—dc23   2011014424

Manufactured in the United States of America
1 – DP – 12/31/11

Jodie dreamed of being a famous archaeologist like her dad. And with the new flashlight she got as a reward for finding the afikomen, she couldn't wait to start. Maybe her cousin Zach would help her uncover treasures hidden deep inside the earth.

"Hey Zach," said Jodie's brother Shimi, "since you're only here for Passover week, let's go skateboarding tomorrow in Liberty Bell Park."

"Great!" said Zach.

"And Wednesday, we'll go biking through the Jerusalem Forest," said Eli, her other brother.

"Sounds good," said Zach.

"Hey, when do I get a turn to be with Zach?" Jodie asked. "He's my cousin, too."

"I'm not sure Zach wants to crawl around underground where there's nothing to see but mutant monsters," said Shimi.

"Archaeologists don't believe in monsters," said Jodie. "Besides, I'll have my new flashlight. And Dad's been promising to take me to Hezekiah's Tunnel."

"Heze who?" asked Zach.

"Hez-uh-KI-ya," said Jodie. "He was King of Jerusalem a long time ago. He even invited all the rulers of Judea to a Passover seder in Jerusalem."

"But he was best known for his water tunnel," Eli said.

"A secret water tunnel," said Shimi, "built to keep the City of Jerusalem safe in case of an enemy attack."

"Under the ground?" asked Zach.

"Deep down," said Shimi, "where it's cold and wet and smelly."

"Archaeologists don't feel the cold," said Jodie. "And they're not afraid of tunnels that smell bad."

"And it's very, very dark," said Eli.

"Archaeologists are not afraid of the dark," said Jodie. "Especially archaeologists with brand new flashlights."

On Thursday, Jodie woke up early. She made matzah sandwiches with jam and butter and packed a box of chocolate macaroons. Zach filled up the water bottles. Digger brought his leash.

Dad drove into the Old City of Jerusalem and parked outside Dung Gate, where his students were working on an archaeological dig.

"So what are we looking for?" asked Zach. "Gold coins? Arrowheads? Jewels?"

"Sometimes it's not what you find, but what you find out," said Dad.

Zach scouted around. He saw jagged stones
that were once foundations for the great walls of the Temple. In the distance he saw
modern houses dotted with satellite antennas. He saw grapevines, and clotheslines, and
pomegranate trees, but no pool, tunnel, or waterway. "Where is the tunnel?" he asked.

"Under here," said Jodie, stomping her foot on the ground.

Dad stopped at the entrance. "Let's see if you two can figure out the 'riddle of the middle.'
Digger and I will meet you at the other end."

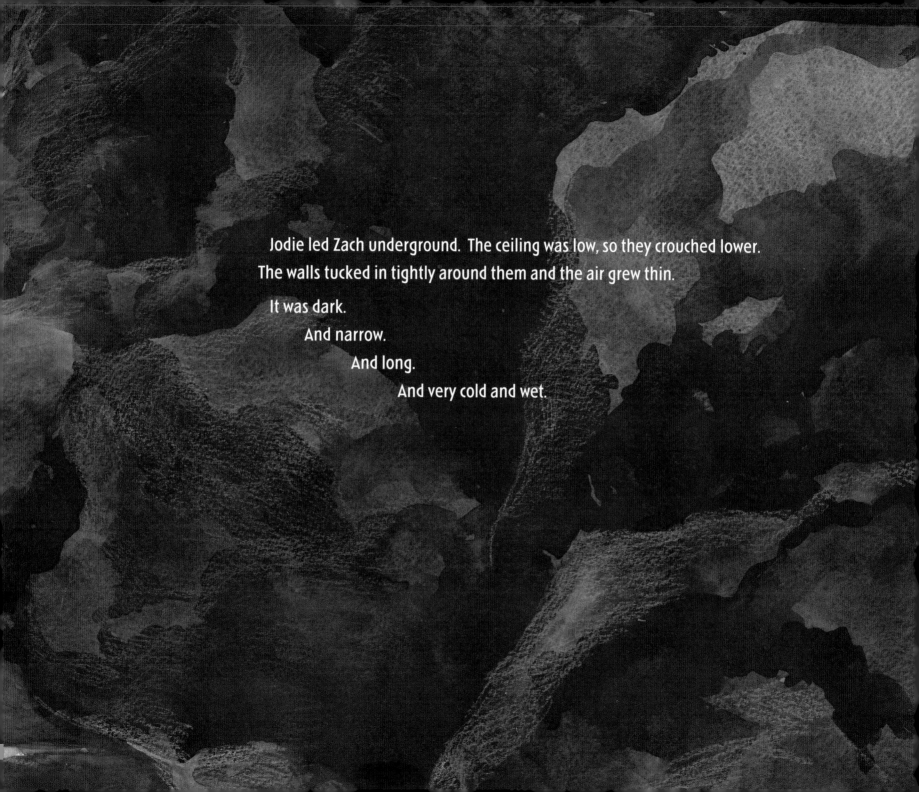

Jodie led Zach underground. The ceiling was low, so they crouched lower.
The walls tucked in tightly around them and the air grew thin.

It was dark.

And narrow.

And long.

And very cold and wet.

"Smell's like dragon breath." Zach pinched his nose. "You don't suppose that there might still be–"

"Mold," Jodie said, touching the dank wall. She handed him a Passover mint.

"Mutant monsters!" exclaimed Zach.

"Shadows," said Jodie. She flicked her flashlight twice, and the monsters disappeared.

"I think I feel dinosaur claws," said Zach, sliding his hand along the wall.

"Dinosaurs lived way before King Hezekiah," said Jodie. She shined her flashlight close to the wall, where long narrow scratches left deep slices in the rock. "Chisel marks," she said. "There were no bulldozers back then. The workers used chisels to tunnel their way through."

"But look, Jodie," he whispered, still unconvinced, "the scratches change direction here."

"Maybe some of the workers started digging from the water spring outside the city, and the others started from inside the city," Jodie suggested.

"And this is where they met—right in the middle. That's amazing!" said Zach. "How could they build it without flashlights or maps to guide them? It's incredible."

"Seems impossible," said Jodie.

"That's the riddle of the middle!" said Zach. "The diggers couldn't believe they really did it— they met right here!" He jumped so high that he bumped his head and slipped, landing with a splash.

"Are you okay?" asked Jodie.

Zach got up slowly. "I think I found a treasure," he said, holding out a wet coin.

Jodie shined her flashlight on it. It was too bumpy and too big to be a shekel. "My dad said that some old coins have been found around here. Maybe this one got swept inside the tunnel by the water."

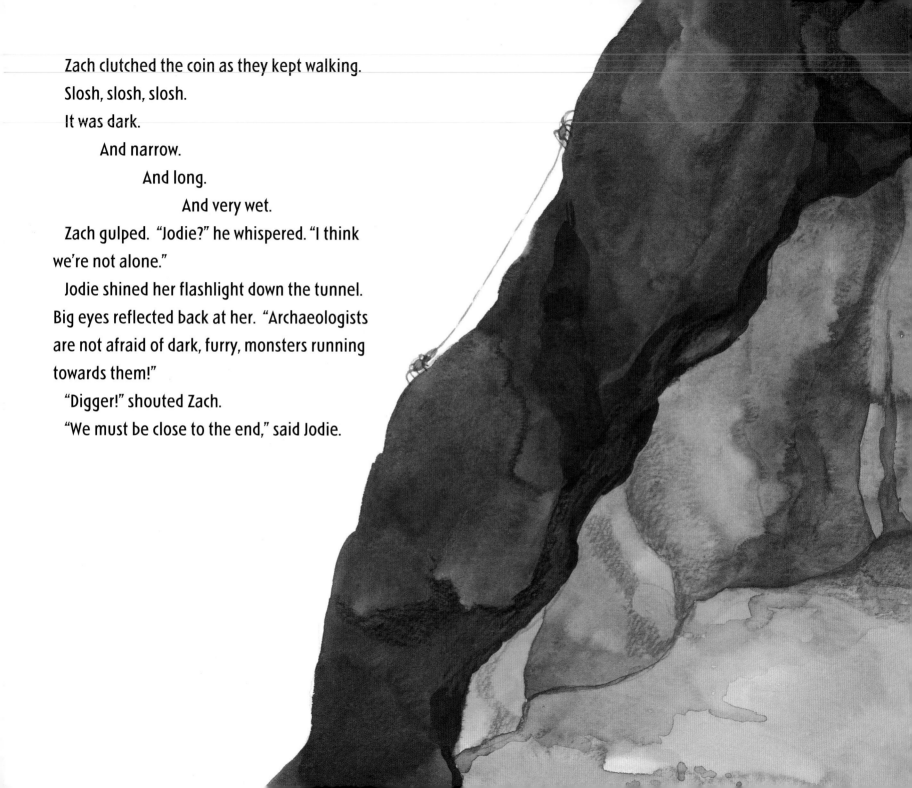

Zach clutched the coin as they kept walking.

Slosh, slosh, slosh.

It was dark.

And narrow.

And long.

And very wet.

Zach gulped. "Jodie?" he whispered. "I think we're not alone."

Jodie shined her flashlight down the tunnel. Big eyes reflected back at her. "Archaeologists are not afraid of dark, furry, monsters running towards them!"

"Digger!" shouted Zach.

"We must be close to the end," said Jodie.

Jodie and Zach followed as Digger splashed his way forward. When they reached the end they were met by a burst of sunlight.

"We made it!" said Jodie, when she saw her dad. "And Zach found an ancient coin."
"And we solved the 'riddle of the middle,'" said Zach.

While Jodie and Zach dried off, Dad wrapped the coin carefully and put it in his pocket. "My students will be excited to see this find," he said.

Then Dad and Zach, and Jodie and Digger sat down to share their Passover picnic.

About the Author and Illustrator

Anna Levine is the author of the children's book *Jodie's Hanukkah Dig* as well as two young adult novels, *Running on Eggs* and *Freefall*. All of her books take place in Israel. Her short stories, poems and non-fiction have appeared in Spider, Cricket and Cicada magazines. "My two 'Jodie' stories reflect my love of archaeology and the excitement of living in a country where history is at our fingertips," says Anna. She lives with her husband and two children in Mevesseret Zion a neighborhood just outside of Jerusalem.

Born in Moscow, **Ksenia Topaz** moved to Israel in 1991. A graduate of Moscow's Strogonoff Academy of Art, Ksenia comes from a family of artists and sculptors. She has illustrated over 20 books including *Jodie's Hanukkah Dig*. The mother of two daughters, Ksenia lives in Jerusalem.